GIANT TURTLE's Long Nap

A Jataka Tale
Retold by Dana Green
Illustrated by Levendivin

Instilling Goodness Books

GIANT TURTLE's
Long Nap

A Jataka Tale
A fictionalized version of "The Tortoise King," Human Roots, Buddhist Text Translation Society, 1982

Retold by Dana Green
Illustrated and designed by Amandine Dam-Levendivin

Published by Instilling Goodness Books
Imprint of Buddhist Text Translation Society
4951 Bodhi Way, Ukiah, CA 95482
www.buddhisttexts.org

Buddhist Text Translation Society
4951 Bodhi Way, Ukiah, CA 95482

www.buddhisttexts.org

info@buddhisttexts.org

Library of Congress Cataloguing-in-Publication Data

Names: Green, Dana, 1942- author. | Levendivin, illustrator.
Title: Giant turtle's long nap : A Jataka tale / retold by Dana ;
    illustrated by Levendivin.
Other titles: Tipiṭaka. Suttapiṭaka. Khuddakanikāya. Jātaka.
    Kacchapajātaka. Paraphrases, English.
Description: First. | Ukiah : Instilling Goodness Books, 2022. | Audience:
    Grades 2-3 | Summary: "A giant turtle teaches patience and sacrifice by
    allowing people and animals to live on his shell upon which a mountain
    had grown during a thousand-year nap"-- Provided by publisher.
Identifiers: LCCN 2021022336 | ISBN 9781642170504 (hardcover)
Subjects: LCSH: Turtles--Juvenile fiction. | Jataka stories,
    English--Juvenile literature.
Classification: LCC BQ1470.K3322 E64 2022 | DDC 294.3/82325--dc23
LC record available at https://lccn.loc.gov/2021022336

The Giant Turtle's Nap is a retelling of a Jataka tale—ancient tales that the Buddha told about his past lives.

In this tale, the Buddha appears as a giant king turtle to teach that all beings are a living part of the earth. Only by developing empathy with each other and all of earth's creatures, can we protect our planet.

The image of the world being carried on the back of a giant turtle has appeared in cultures across the globe from ancient times. In many Native myths, North America was created on the back of a giant turtle who continues to carry it today. Modern Natives call it Turtle Island.

Today, giant sea turtles who have reigned over the oceans for 150 million years are struggling to survive and need our help and compassion. By working together, we can hopefully save the turtles and create a positive future for the earth.

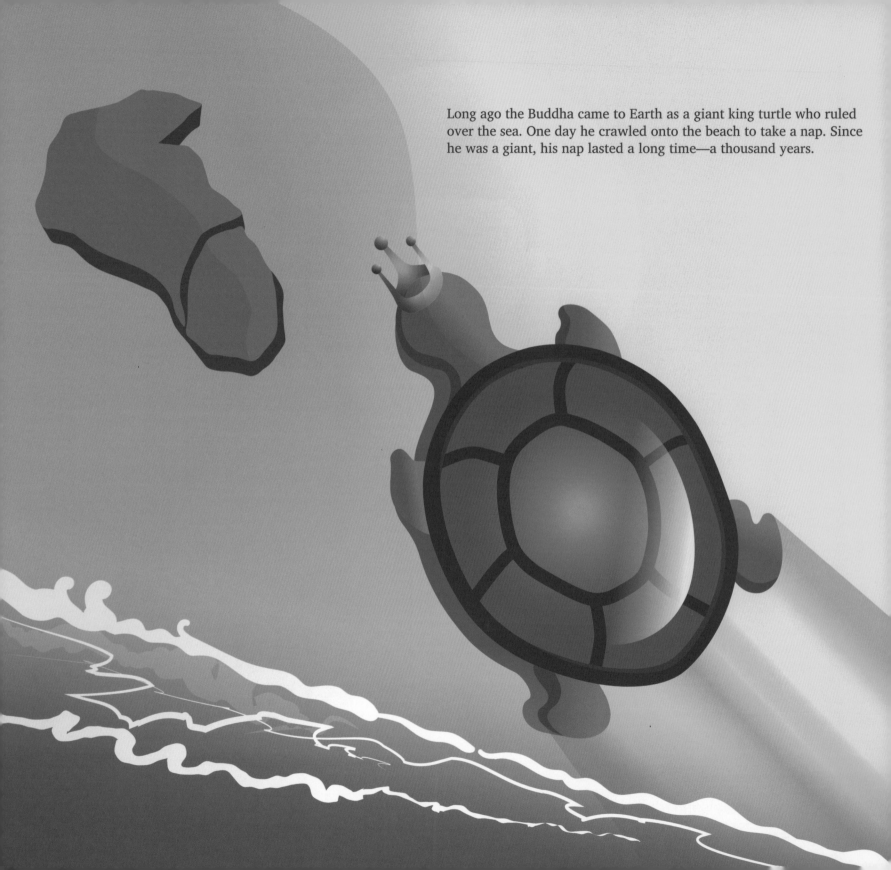

Long ago the Buddha came to Earth as a giant king turtle who ruled over the sea. One day he crawled onto the beach to take a nap. Since he was a giant, his nap lasted a long time—a thousand years.

In the nights the rains came dropping tiny raindrops
onto the turtle's back.

Drip, drop! Drip, drop!

The raindrops flowed
down between the
grooves on the turtle's
shell, forming rivers and
lakes.

The turtle slept on.

In the mornings the winds came up, blowing tiny grains of sand onto the turtle's back. *Whoo-sha! Whoo-sha!* The sand grains joined together forming mountains and valleys.

The turtle slept on.

In the afternoons birds flew over, dropping tiny seeds onto his back. Plink! Plink! The seeds sprouted, and there on the turtle's back grew trees and flowers and grass.

The turtle slept on.

The sun warmed him through the days.

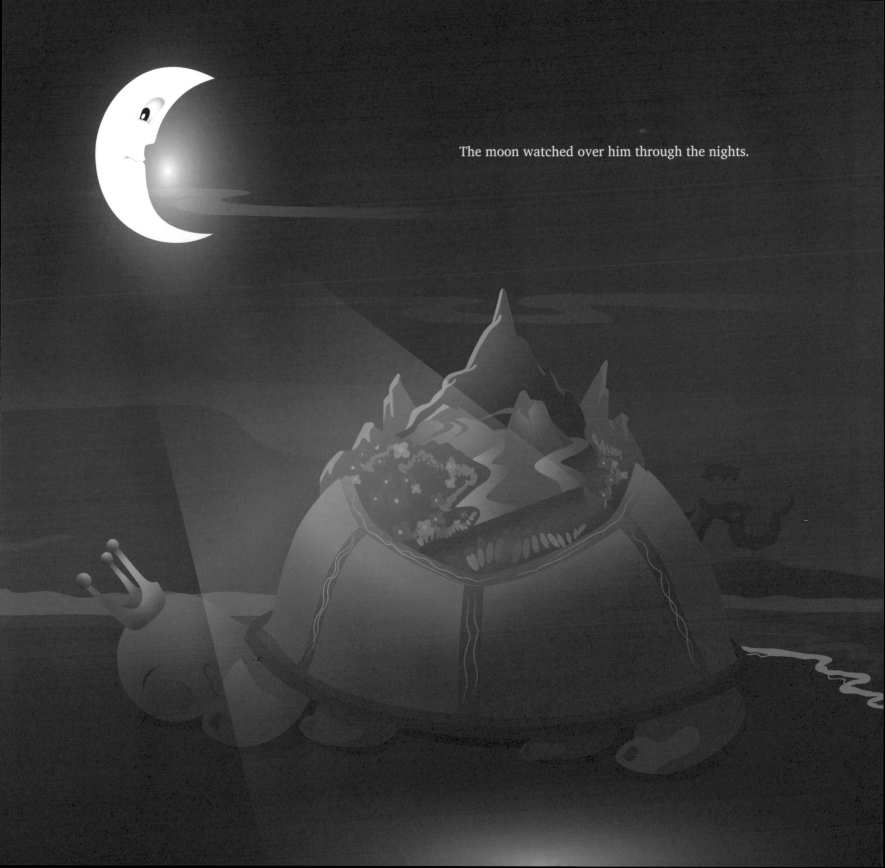

The moon watched over him through the nights.

Time passed and the seasons embraced the giant turtle with spring, summer, autumn, and winter.

And all that lived on the turtle's back experienced the seasons and multiplied.

One day a child wandered onto the mountain to pick wildflowers.

The next day she returned with her family. Her father said,
"This will be a good place to build a house."

The next year another family moved to the little mountain, then another.
Roads were built and merchants set up shops.

A prince built a palace.

And the turtle slept on.

People pulled their carts and rode their carriages over the streets, cutting deep ruts into the turtle's shell. Their cities became a burden on his back. Their noises rumbled in his ears and their fires burned his skin.

And so it went until one day the giant turtle was awakened by the pain from the fires and began to crawl toward the sea to cool off. **EARTHQUAKE! EARTHQUAKE!** cried the people.

For the first time, the giant turtle realized that there were people living on his back. Not wanting to hurt them, he took another nap for another thousand years.

He let the fires burn his skin and the rumbling carts shake him. In the day he held back the tears, but in the night he let them flow. So great was his pain and so silent were his tears—no one knew of his sacrifice.

At last, the giant turtle could take no more. He raised his head and said to the people, "Don't be afraid. I won't hurt you. I'm a giant turtle, and you're living on my shell. I must go back into the sea or I will die."

"But where will we live?' cried the people. "Our ancestors have
 lived on this mountain for two thousand years."

"I have no idea," said the turtle.
"I haven't had a thought for two thousand years, so I need to think."

The people waited,...

Then he smiled and said, "I remember an island with rivers and mountains and trees and flowers. I will take you there."

The giant turtle eased the people and their homes and the palace off his back. The people would create new villages and cities on the island, and their lives would go on as before.

Birds placed garlands of flowers around the turtle's neck. Monkeys rubbed his sores with herbs. Elephants trumpeted sweet music to soothe his ears. And people swept the dirt from his back.

Their songs of gratitude followed the giant turtle as he crawled back into his kingdom in the sea. And since he was a giant, he would not need a nap for another thousand years.

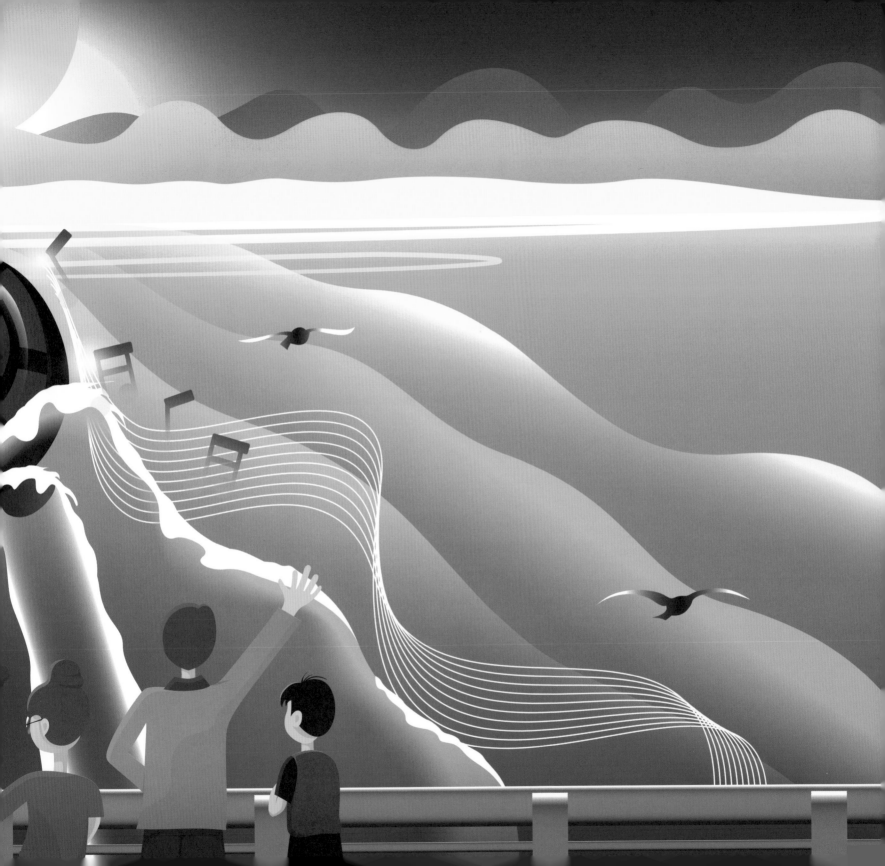

SEA TURTLES ARE IMPORTANT

1. Sea turtles graze on seagrass and keep the oceans clean and heathy.
2. They eat sponges so the coral reefs can grow.
3. They feast on jellyfish to keep a balance, so other fish won't disappear.
4. Their shells are homes for barnacles, crabs, and shrimp.
5. Their backs are perches where birds can land and rest at sea.
6. They are umbrellas for sea creatures to hide for safety.
7. They provide jobs for people: turtle watching, diving, and ecotourism.
8. They may get caught in fishing gear and need your help.

WAYS TO HELP SEA TURTLES

1. Say no to plastic! Turtles may confuse plastic bags and balloons for food and eat them, causing injury or death.
2. Pick up litter and keep the beaches clean.
3. Use eco-friendly products. Chemical products wash into the sea, killing plants and animals.
4. Keep nesting beaches dark and safe for hatchlings.
5. Watch out for turtles when boating. They often get entangled in fishing gear and may need your help.
6. Avoid eating turtle eggs and meat. Do not buy items made from turtle shells and skin.
7. Volunteer! Organize clean-up days. Talk to others about how to save our turtles.

Please visit our websites:
www.buddhisttexts.org and www.buddhismforkids.net

INSTILLING GOODNESS BOOKS offers beautifully illustrated books to share the Buddha's teachings with children, in different languages. The growing collection includes a series of delightful books on kindness to animals and respect for the earth. The authors, illustrators, and designers of our books are inspired by the Buddha's teaching and the guidance and wisdom of the late Venerable Master Hsuan Hua.